CLASSIC FAIRY TALES
Donkey Skin

Written by Barbara Hayes

Illustrated by Jesus Blasco

Library of Congress Cataloging in Publication Data

Hayes, Barbara, 1944-
  Donkey skin.

  (Classic fairy tales)
  Summary: A lovely princess flees from impending
marriage with a king, donning a donkey skin, and goes to
live on a poor farm where she eventually sights a handsome
prince.
  [1. Fairy tales. 2. Folklore—France] I. Blasco,
Jesus, ill. II. Title. III. Series.
PZ8.H325 1984   [398.2] [E]   84-11461
ISBN 0-86592-226-8

ROURKE ENTERPRISES, INC.
Vero Beach, Florida 32964

CLASSIC FAIRY TALES
Donkey Skin

Once upon a time a young and beautiful princess was left without father or mother. She was brought up by an old friend of her father.

This friend was king of a large country. He always wore a donkey skin coat. One day the king said to her: "Miranda, if you marry me, you will be rich and important. Are you pleased?" Poor Miranda!

The king was old and ugly. Miranda did not want to marry him. She hoped to marry a young man. Princess Miranda went to see her fairy godmother. She asked for advice.

6

"The king must not be offended," said the fairy. "Do not refuse to marry him. Find ways to delay the wedding day,"
The princess asked for a dress the color of the sky.

Finding material to make a dress
the color of the sky took a long
time. At last the dress was finished.
Princess Miranda wore the dress to
dance with the king. She felt
unhappy. Now she would have to
marry this old man.

That night the princess went to a cave. Her fairy godmother lived there. "What shall I do?" asked the princess.

"Tell the king you need another pretty dress before you can get married," the fairy godmother said.

This time the princess asked for a dress the color of the moon. It had to be made from silver thread. It took a long time to make.

At last the dress was finished. "You look lovely," said the king. "Now you have such pretty  clothes, we can get married." Miranda nodded. Miranda still did not want to marry the old king. Again she went to visit her fairy godmother to ask advice.

"Ask for a dress of gold and
diamonds," advised the fairy. "The
king will be angry at such
greediness. He will not want to
marry you." Princess Miranda asked
for a dress of gold and diamonds.
The king was not angry. He gave
her the dress. It was lovely.

Again the
princess ran
out of the
palace. She
went to see
the fairy.
"You must
ask the king

for something he will never give

you," she
said to
Miranda.

Princess
Miranda
stood before
the king. "I
will marry
you if you will give me your coat
of donkey skin," she said.
Everyone knew the donkey skin
coat brought the king good luck.
He would never give it to anyone.
To her amazement, the king gave
the coat to the princess. Now she
would have to marry him.

Princess Miranda decided to run away. She put her three pretty dresses into a magic box. She waved a wand

and the box disappeared. Only Miranda knew she had it.

Princess Miranda walked
for many miles. She wore
the donkey skin coat so she would
not look like a princess.
She came to a farm. She was given
work in the kitchen.

One day a handsome prince rode by. He took no notice of Miranda in her rags. She was upset. She went indoors and put on one of her pretty dresses.

The young man saw her.
The prince thought he was bewitched to see a grand lady  in a back room at such a poor farm. He went home and went to bed. He would not eat. Everyone heard of the prince's illness.
Miranda baked a cake and put a magic ring in it.

She took the
cake to
the palace
and said
it would
cure the
prince.
The prince
ate the cake
and found
the magic ring.
He told his
Prime Minister
to announce
that he would
marry the
girl whose
finger fitted
the ring.

To everyone's surprise, the ring fitted the poor servant girl they called Donkey Skin.

Donkey Skin was Princess Miranda. She put on one of her pretty dresses.

Now Miranda looked like a princess again. The prince married her. The old king promised never to bother her again. She was happy.

Test your memory

Read the story first. Then try to answer these questions.

Who brought up Miranda? (Page 4)

To whom did she go for help? (Page 6)

What did the King always wear? (Page 5)

To whom did he give it? (Page 14)

After each question is the page number where you will find the answer.

What made the Prince fall ill? (Page 18)

What was in his cake? (Page 19)

Who is this man? (Page 19)

What did the Prince tell him to do? (Page 19)